Cat Club

Sphynx

by Cameron L. Woodson

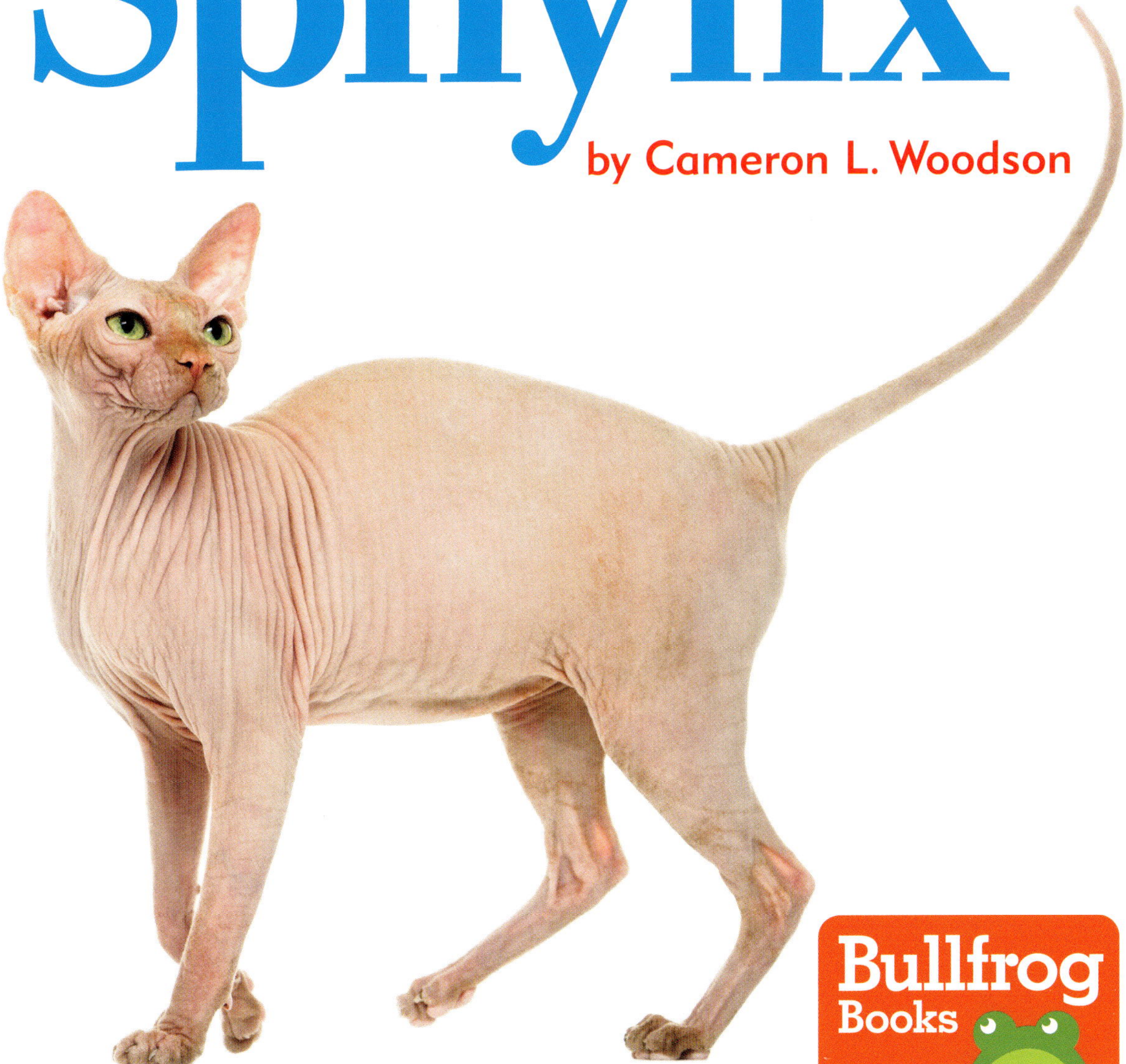

Bullfrog Books

Ideas for Parents and Teachers

Bullfrog Books let children practice reading informational text at the earliest reading levels. Repetition, familiar words, and photo labels support early readers.

Before Reading

- Discuss the cover photo. What does it tell them?
- Look at the picture glossary together. Read and discuss the words.

Read the Book

- "Walk" through the book and look at the photos. Let the child ask questions. Point out the photo labels.
- Read the book to the child, or have him or her read independently.

After Reading

- Prompt the child to think more. Ask: Sphynx cats have almost no fur! Can you think of other animals that don't have any fur?

Bullfrog Books are published by Jump!
5357 Penn Avenue South
Minneapolis, MN 55419
www.jumplibrary.com

Library of Congress Cataloging-in-Publication Data

Names: Woodson, Cameron L., 1994– author.
Title: Sphynx / Cameron L. Woodson.
Description: Minneapolis: Jump!, Inc., [2021]
Series: Cat club | Includes index.
Audience: Ages 5–8
Identifiers: LCCN 2019049896 (print)
LCCN 2019049897 (ebook)
ISBN 9781645274575 (hardcover)
ISBN 9781645274582 (ebook)
Subjects: LCSH: Sphynx cat—Juvenile literature.
Classification: LCC SF449.S68 W66 2021 (print)
LCC SF449.S68 (ebook)
DDC 636.8—dc23
LC record available at https://lccn.loc.gov/2019049896
LC ebook record available at
https://lccn.loc.gov/2019049897

Editors: Jenna Gleisner and Susanne Bushman
Designer: Jenna Casura

Photo Credits: Eric Isselee/Shutterstock, cover, 1, 3, 24; Andrii Spy_k/Shutterstock, 4; New Africa/Shutterstock, 5, 23 tm; Casey Elise Christopher/Shutterstock, 6–7; Triff/Shutterstock, 8–9, 23tr; Kucher Serhii/Shutterstock, 10, 23br; Nils Jacobi/Shutterstock, 11, 23bl; Stephen Jingel/Shutterstock, 12–13; GlobalP/iStock, 14, 22; JPR03/Shutterstock, 15 (foreground); hanohiki/Shutterstock, 15 (background); Cavan Images/Getty, 16–17, 23tl; everytime/Shutterstock, 18–19, 23bm; FXQuadro/Shutterstock, 20–21 (foreground); ben bryant/Shutterstock, 20–21 (background).

Printed in the United States of America at Corporate Graphics in North Mankato, Minnesota.

Table of Contents

Wrinkly Wonders

This is a Sphynx!

You can see its skin.

Why?

It has almost no fur!

sweater

These cats can get cold.

This one wears a sweater!

These cats look bald.
But they do have fuzz.

fuzz

They have wrinkles.

Their skin can be oily.
We give ours a bath!
Nice!

They can be many colors.

This one is black!

Their heads are small.

But their ears are big!

Wow!

Their tails are long.
They are thin.

These cats are active.

They love to play!

Fun!

perch

They like to be up high.
Mine likes its perch.
Cool!

Would you like a Sphynx?

A Sphynx Up Close

A Sphynx has almost no fur. It has a small head, large ears, and a long, thin tail. See its other body parts!

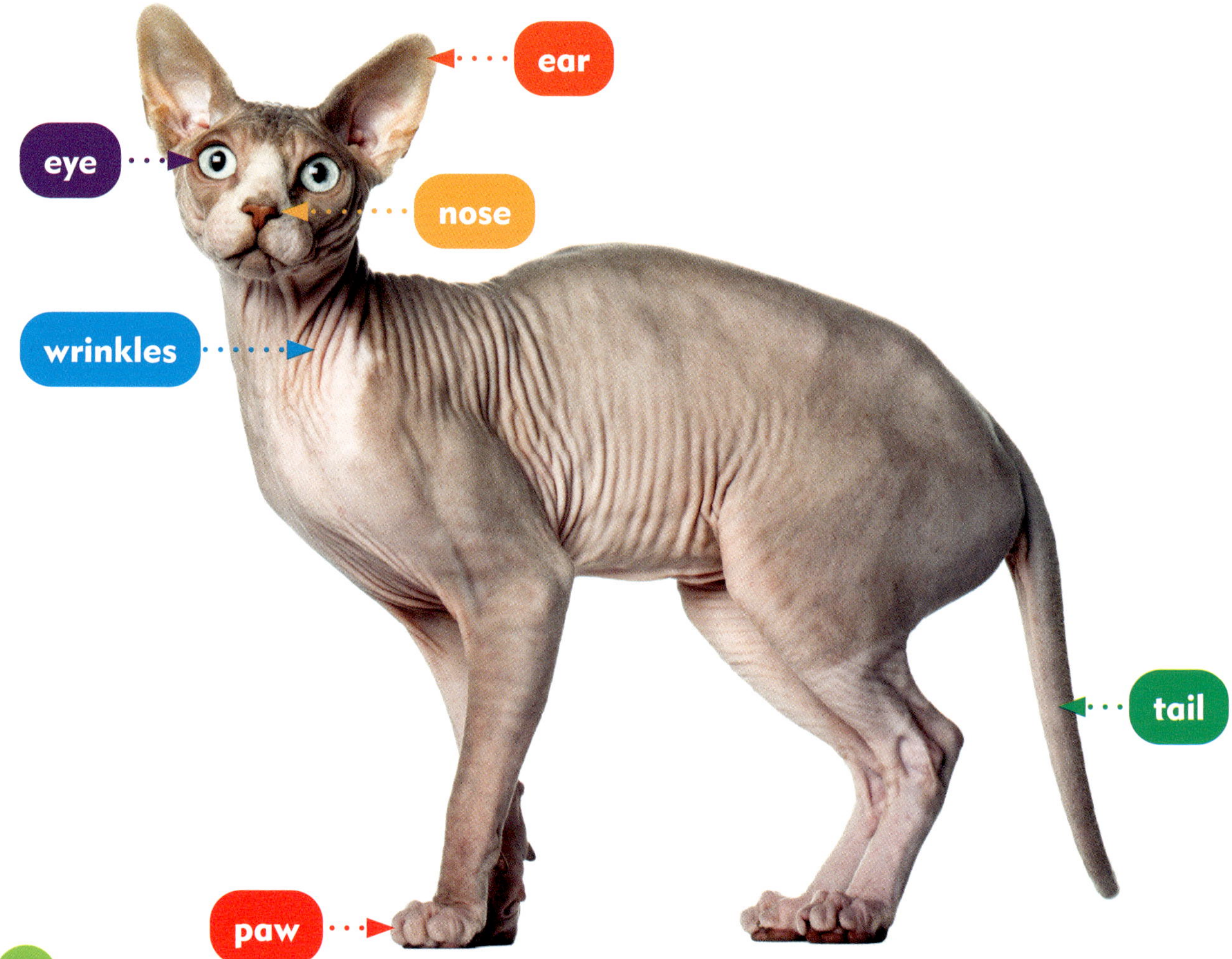

Picture Glossary

active
Energetic and busy.

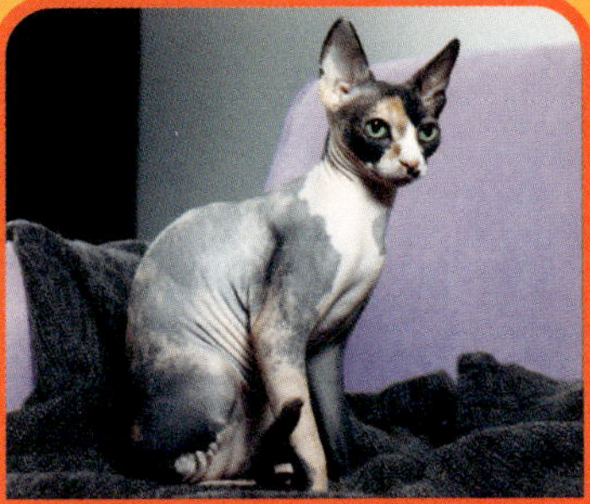

bald
Having little or no fur.

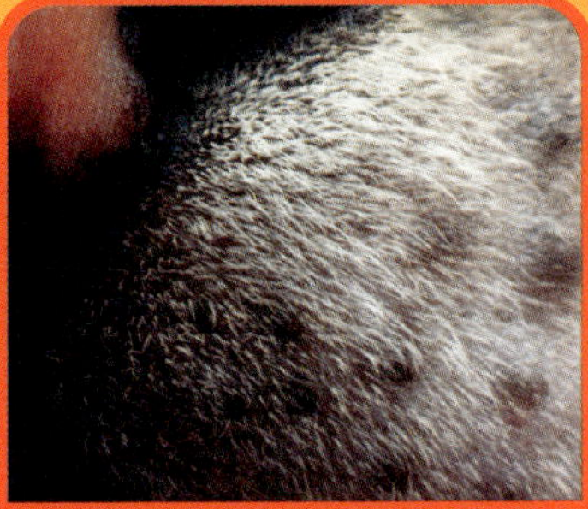

fuzz
A coating of short, soft fur.

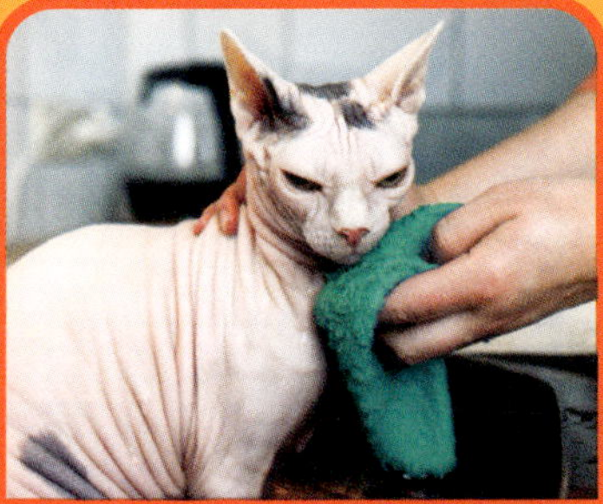

oily
Producing a greasy liquid.

perch
A raised place where a cat can sit.

wrinkles
Folds in the skin.

Index

To Learn More

Finding more information is as easy as 1, 2, 3.

1. Go to www.factsurfer.com
2. Enter "Sphynx" into the search box.
3. Click the "Surf" button to see a list of websites.